Oliver
Great Western

Based on *The Railway Series* by the Rev. W. Awdry

Illustrations by *Robin Davies and Jerry Smith*

EGMONT

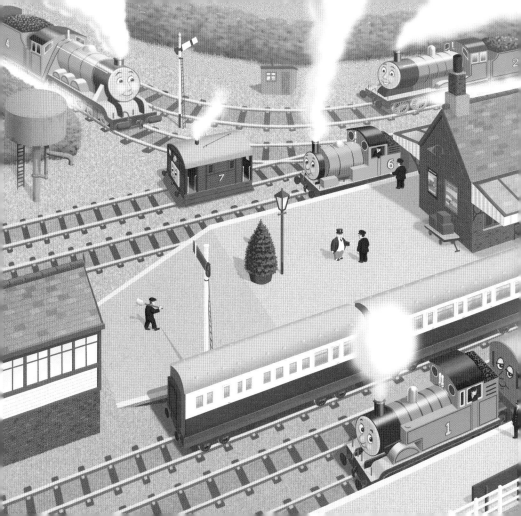

EGMONT

We bring stories to life

First published in Great Britain 2004
This edition published in 2011
by Egmont UK Limited
239 Kensington High Street, London W8 6SA

Thomas the Tank Engine & Friends™

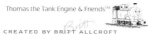

CREATED BY BRITT ALLCROFT

Based on the Railway Series by the Reverend W Awdry
© 2011 Gullane (Thomas) LLC. A HIT Entertainment company.
Thomas the Tank Engine & Friends and Thomas & Friends are trademarks of Gullane (Thomas) Limited.
Thomas the Tank Engine & Friends and Design is Reg. U.S. Pat. & Tm. Off.

HiT entertainment

ISBN 978 1 4052 3460 3
42492/20
Printed in Italy

FSC
MIX
Paper
FSC® C018306

Egmont is passionate about helping to preserve the world's remaining ancient forests.
We only use paper from legal and sustainable forest sources.

This book is made from paper certified by the Forestry Stewardship Council (FSC),
an organisation dedicated to promoting responsible management of forest resources.
For more information on the FSC, please visit www.fsc.org. To learn more about
Egmont's sustainable paper policy, please visit www.egmont.co.uk/ethical

TO THE TRAINS ➡

This is a story about Oliver the Great Western Engine. His owner didn't want him any more and he was going to be turned into scrap. Then someone came to the rescue . . .

One day, Edward was talking to Douglas. They had heard that steam engines were being put out of service across the Island and replaced by new diesel engines.

"They're being turned into scrap," said Edward quietly.

"Don't mention that word!" Douglas gasped. "It makes my wheels wobble."

"I agree," replied Edward. "But The Fat Controller says he will make sure there are always steam engines on his Railway."

"I'm glad we work for The Fat Controller," smiled Douglas.

That night, Douglas was still working. He had taken the Midnight Goods Train to a station at a far away part of the Island, where only the diesels worked. He was just shunting ready for his return journey, when he heard a faint hiss.

"That sounds like a steam engine," he thought in surprise.

The hiss came again.

"Who's there?" asked Douglas.

"I'm Oliver," whispered a voice. "Are you one of The Fat Controller's engines?"

"Aye, and proud of it," replied Douglas.

"Thank goodness!" said the voice. In the darkness, Douglas could just make out a little Western Engine. "This is my coach, Isabel and brake van, Toad, " said the engine. "We've run out of coal and I have no more steam."

"But, what are you doing here?" asked Douglas.

"Escaping from the scrap yard," replied Oliver, trembling.

Douglas shivered. "I'll be glad to help you," he said. "We'll make it look as though you're ready for scrap and I'm taking you away."

The Driver and Fireman agreed to help, too. Everyone worked fast. They took off Oliver's side-rods, wrote out transit labels saying that he belonged to The Fat Controller, and chalked 'SCRAP' all over him.

"Nay time for me to turn around," panted Douglas. "I will have to run backwards."

Douglas and Oliver started out on their journey. But before they could leave the station, they were stopped.

"Aha!" exclaimed a Foreman, shining his torch at Oliver. "A Great Western Engine!" His light flickered further back. "With a Western coach, and a brake van! You can't take these."

"But they're all for us. See for yourself," exclaimed Douglas' Driver.

Douglas' Driver showed him the transit labels. Oliver and Douglas hardly dared to breathe.

The Foreman looked all over Oliver.
"Seems in order. You can go, Driver," he said.

"Phew! That was a near thing," puffed Douglas.

"We've had worse," smiled Oliver. "We were nearly caught getting here and had to hide on an old quarry branch for three days. I was very frightened."

"I'm not surprised," replied Douglas. And they forged ahead.

It was daylight when their journey ended.

"We're home!" cried Douglas as they reached The Fat Controller's Railway. "I know just the place for you." And he showed them an empty siding, nicely hidden away.

"Goodbye and thank you," whispered Oliver.

"I was happy to help," smiled Douglas, and he puffed away.

Back at the shed, Douglas told the other engines all about Oliver. They were very excited, and agreed that something must be done for him.

"The Fat Controller will have to know," said James.

"Douglas should tell him at once," added Gordon firmly.

"Well, here I am," said a cheerful voice. "Now, what all this about?"

It was The Fat Controller! The engines were silent.

"Beg your pardon, Sir, but we do need another engine," said Duck quietly, at last.

"Yes Sir, a steam engine Sir," said Gordon.

"We do indeed!" replied The Fat Controller. "But I'm afraid that unless one is saved from scrap, there's little hope."

"But Sir," burst out Douglas, "one has been!"

"Who told you that, Douglas?" asked The Fat Controller.

The engines looked nervously at each other.

"Sir, er . . . I saved him," muttered Douglas.

"You saved a steam engine?" exclaimed The Fat Controller. "I want to hear everything!"

So Douglas told him all about how he had rescued Oliver, Isabel and Toad from the scrap yard. When he had finished, The Fat Controller smiled.

"I'm proud of you, Douglas," he said. "Oliver, Isabel and Toad are just what we need for Duck's branch line."

"Thank you, Sir!" replied Douglas.

And all the engines cheered.

The Fat Controller soon had Oliver, Isabel and Toad mended and painted in full Great Western colours. They are very happy on Duck's branch line.

As Oliver puffs along the coast, he often thinks about what a lucky escape he had. If Douglas hadn't come to the rescue things would be very different. Oliver is very grateful to Douglas and everyone at The Fat Controller's Railway for his lovely new home!

Thomas Story Library

 Thomas

 Edward

 Henry

 Gordon

 James

 Percy

 Toby

 Emily

 Alfie

 Annie and Clarabel

 'Arry and Bert

 Arthur

 Bertie

 Bill and Ben

Peep! Peep!

 BoCo

 Bulgy

 Charlie

 Cranky

 Daisy

 Dennis

 Diesel

 Donald and Douglas

Duck

 Duncan

 The Fat Controller

 Fergus

 Freddie

 George

 Harold

 Hector

 Hiro

 Jack

 Jeremy

 Kevin

 Mighty Mac

 Murdoch

 Oliver

 Peter Sam

 Rocky

 Rosie

 Rusty

 Salty

 Sir Handel

 Skarloey

 Spencer

 Stepney

 Terence

 Trevor

 Troublesome Trucks

 Victor